ME GUSTA

Angela Dominguez

Henry Holt and Company

New York

Henry Holt and Company, *Publishers since 1866*
Henry Holt® is a registered trademark of Macmillan Publishing Group, LLC
120 Broadway, New York, NY 10271 · mackids.com

Copyright © 2022 by Angela Dominguez

Our books may be purchased in bulk for promotional, educational, or business use. Please contact your local bookseller or the Macmillan Corporate
and Premium Sales Department at (800) 221-7945 ext. 5442 or by email at MacmillanSpecialMarkets@macmillan.com.

Library of Congress Cataloging-in-Publication Data is available.

First edition, 2022
Book design by Ashley Caswell
Printed in China by Hung Hing Off-set Printing Co. Ltd., Heshan City, Guangdong Province

ISBN 978-1-250-81854-6 (hardcover)
1 3 5 7 9 10 8 6 4 2

For my family
Para mi familia

Mi corazón, **my heart,**

there is so much que me gusta.

Like running through
the sprinklers with you.

Or eating ice cream, el helado, together before it melts.

Me gusta **your smile**, tu sonrisa,
and **your hugs**, tus abrazos.

Me gustan **our**
family traditions.

las tradiciones . . .

Our stories, los cuentos,

both
imaginary
and real.

But there are things que no me gustan.

No me gustan **mean words.**

las palabras malas.

No me gusta **prejudice toward**

our beautiful skin, nuestra piel hermosa.

No me gusta when you feel sad,
triste, and alone, solo.

But me gusta when we listen to each other . . .

. . . and when we work to

Me gusta when we explore
this spectacular world,
el mundo . . .

. . . and gaze at all the stars. las estrellas.

But most of all, me gusta that no matter where we are,

I feel at home, en casa, when I'm with you.

Te quiero.
I love you.